THE INCREDIBLE DINOSAUR EXPEDITION

Karen Dolby

Illustrated by
Brenda Haw

Designed by Patrick Knowles

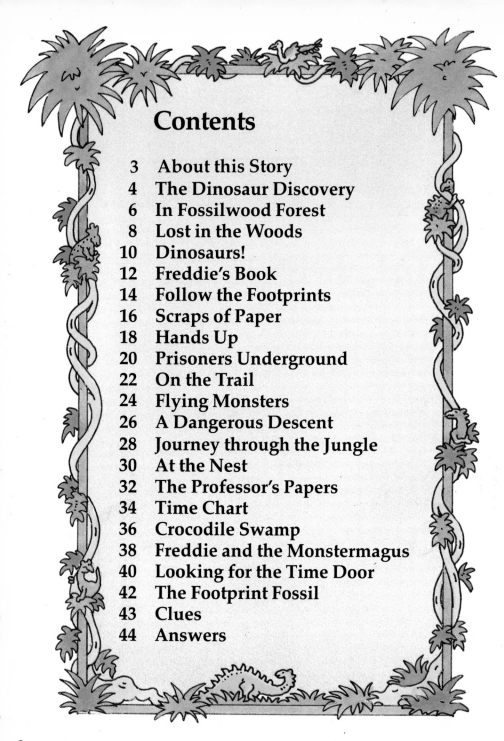

Contents

About this Story

The Incredible Dinosaur Expedition is an action-packed adventure story that takes you backwards in time to the eerie, unknown world of the dinosaurs.

Along the way, there are lots of fun puzzles and tricky problems to solve. Find the answers to these before going on to the next episode in the story.

Look at the picture carefully and watch out for vital clues and information. Sometimes you will need to flip back through the story to help you find an answer.

There are extra clues on page 43 and you can check your answers on pages 44 to 48.

Just turn the page to begin the adventure . . .

The Dinosaur Discovery

Freddie was bored, so bored that he had even lent Jo his roller skates. He munched his way through a bag of banana toffees and wished that something exciting would happen.

Just then, Freddie's friend, Zack, zoomed up on his skateboard.

"Come and read this," Zack yelled, waving a very crumpled newspaper page.

"But newspapers are so boring," Freddie groaned, aiming a toffee at Zack's head.

"There's been the most amazing dinosaur discovery," said Zack, ignoring Freddie.

"And it's near here," Jo exclaimed, staring at the page. "In Fossilwood Forest."

"Let's go," said Zack. "Maybe WE can find some dinosaur bones."

Freddie groaned again and carried on munching. But two toffees later he set off after Zack and Jo.

On the right you can read Zack's newspaper.

Jo

Zack

Freddie

4

~DAILY SCOOP~

AMAZING DINOSAUR DISCOVERY
...it's a monster mystery

by Ivor Lead

Late last night, the most incredible dinosaur discovery EVER was made in Fossilwood Forest.

A team of dinosaur experts led by Professor Cuthbert Crank-Pott have found a whole dinosaur skeleton, of a type never seen before.

MONSTERMAGUS

Professor Crank-Pott has named this amazing dinosaur MONSTERMAGUS. In an exclusive interview earlier today, he described the monster.

"This dinosaur was huge – 45 feet tall with large, sharp claws on its feet. It must have devoured enormous amounts of flesh every day and makes Tyrannosaurus Rex look as fierce as a baby hamster."

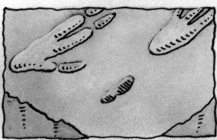

These amazing fossil footprints were found beneath the dinosaur skeleton. The large prints belong to the Monstermagus, but the little one is a mystery. It looks like a human shoeprint.

Humans and dinosaurs never lived on earth together . . . or did they?

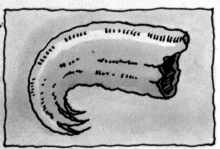

This three-spiked claw belonged to the Monstermagus. It had two of them, one on each of its feet. Experts believe they were used for spearing its prey. So far only one of them has been found.

MYSTERIOUS CLAIMS

On top of his startling skeleton discovery, Professor Crank-Pott claims that he has found a method of hatching live dinosaurs from prehistoric eggs!

He refuses to reveal the secret of his discovery but promises to show the world the results.

Is this really possible? No one knows for sure. A rival expert, Dr Noel Knowall says the Professor's claims are "crazy" "daft" "mad" and "impossible". We shall have to wait and see . . .

Professor Crank-Pott

FOSSILWOOD FOREST LONG AGO

150 million years ago, dinosaurs roamed what is now Fossilwood Forest. No one knows what the landscape looked like then. Some experts say it was a marshy swamp, others think the land was dotted with erupting volcanoes. The Monstermagus and the footprint fossils were buried in a layer of volcanic lava, but nearby, experts have found fossils of shells and prehistoric crocodiles.

In Fossilwood Forest

Half an hour later they stumbled into a clearing in Fossilwood Forest. This was the site of the dinosaur discovery, but it wasn't at all what they expected.

"It looks just like a rubbish dump," moaned Freddie.

Zack and Jo pulled out their spades and started searching through the rubbish for dinosaur bones. Freddie found a comfortable spot beneath a tree and pulled out something plastic and stripey.

"What's that?" cried Zack.

"My inflatable air cushion, of course," said Freddie.

Then, to Zack and Jo's amazement, he blew up the air cushion and sat down with his pocket dinosaur book and a mammoth bar of chocolate.

Jo chucked a slithery earthworm in Freddie's direction and carried on scrabbling in the rubbish. All of a sudden, she spotted something.

"Look! Look over there," she cried in an excited voice. "It's the Monstermagus claw!"

Can you find the missing Monstermagus claw?

Lost in the Woods

Very carefully, Jo pried the claw out of the ground. She wrapped it in Freddie's empty toffee bag and put it in her backpack.

"Let's go home," Freddie said as a raindrop trickled down his neck. "I'm getting wet and this wood is starting to give me the creeps."

The other two agreed. They had to make their way to Forest Lane. But which way was it?

"I know," said Jo. "Take the left fork at the well and . . ."

"No," said Zack. "It's straight on at the well and across the crossroads. First left, first right, right again and first left. Over the bridge and we're there. Easy."

"Wrong," said Jo. "Left at the well and straight on at Hangman's Cross. Follow the path round past the track to Spring Cottage, turn left at the end and take the second path on the right. Then follow the long, wiggly path to Forest Lane."

"You're both wrong," said Freddie. "We go right at Hangman's Cross, follow the path over the bridge, turn second left, then first left and Forest Lane is at the end."

They chose Zack's route and as they walked on through the forest the sky grew darker.

Where does Zack's route take them?
Whose route is correct?

8

St Elmo's Church

Lizard Rock

Stony Brook

Ruined Cottage

Wild Woods

Marlpit

Stone Barn

Old Well

Haunted House

9

Dinosaurs!

All of a sudden they saw a patch of bright light ahead. They hurried towards it and stepped out into hot, hazy sunshine.

Jo stared in amazement. The forest had become a jungle. A giant dragonfly whizzed past Zack's nose and Freddie shrieked as a large, slimy slug slid over his shoes.

But most terrifying of all, were the strange roars and crashes, coming closer and closer. Zack made a gap in the leaves and peered through.

"M . . . m . . . monsters," he gasped.

"No, dinosaurs," gulped Freddie. "Or what look like dinosaurs."

"But . . . how . . ?" Jo began.

Some of the dinosaurs were so near they could hear them chewing. Were THEY going to be eaten next?

"It's all right!" said Freddie, pulling his dinosaur book out of his pocket. "Look, it says here that some dinosaurs only eat plants. They're quite safe. But we must look out for the meat-eaters."

**You can see Freddie's dinosaur book over the page.
Can you work out which dinosaurs eat meat and which eat plants?**

Freddie's Book

Dinosaurs

Dinosaurs were a group of creatures who lived on earth for 135 million years. They died out over 60 million years before man appeared.

The word dinosaur means "terrible lizard". There were lots of different types of dinosaurs and we know what they looked like from fossils, although we don't know what color they were.

Tyrannosaurus Rex

Fossils

A fossil is the remains of an animal or plant preserved in stone. There are fossils of dinosaur bones, eggs, teeth and claws. There are even fossils of their footprints and skin.

A dinosaur became a fossil if its body was buried quickly. This was most likely to happen if it died near water. You can find out how this happened below.

How Fossils Were Made

When a dinosaur died near a swamp or river its body sank into the mud at the bottom. There its flesh rotted away, leaving the skeleton.

Layers of mud, sand and gravel built up. Then chemicals from the water entered the dinosaur's bones, slowly turning the skeleton into rock.

Movements in the earth's crust shift rocks containing fossils to the surface. Wind and rain wear away the rock and uncover part of the fossil.

Footprints

Megalosaurus

Fossil footprints were made when a dinosaur walked on mud which was baked hard by the sun and covered by sand. Slowly this turned into rock with the footprint tracks still in it.

What Dinosaurs Ate

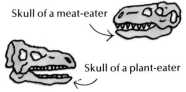

Skull of a meat-eater

Skull of a plant-eater

Some dinosaurs ate meat – they had sharp, pointed teeth. Others ate plants – they had flat, grinding teeth and some had bony beaks.

Bony plates

Spikes

Plant-eaters had to protect themselves from meat-eaters. Some plant-eaters had spikes or bony plates on their bodies, others stayed in herds.

Big and Small

Diplodocus

Compsognathus

Diplodocus was one of the biggest dinosaurs, measuring 28 yards from its head to the tip of its tail. It ate plants and stayed in herds.

The smallest dinosaur, called *Compsognathus*, was only the size of a crow. It ran very fast and ate insects and small reptiles.

Baby Dinosaurs

Baby *Protoceratops*

Most dinosaurs laid eggs. These were buried, or laid in a hollow "nest" in the ground. Fossils of *Protoceratops* eggs, like the ones above, have been found with baby dinosaur bones inside. The babies looked just like small adults.

Follow the Footprints

Zack and Jo didn't wait to look at Freddie's dinosaur book. They turned round and ran back through the bushes, retracing their steps. Freddie followed. Their footprints were clear enough, but everything else was different. Where were they?

"We must have walked through a time warp," Freddie said cheerfully.

"WHAT?" cried Zack and Jo together.

"I think we've travelled backwards in time . . . to the age of the dinosaurs," Freddie explained.

"But they're the wrong color for dinosaurs," said Jo.

"How do you know?" asked Freddie.

They walked on in silence. Zack and Jo tried hard to find another explanation, but they couldn't think of one.

"But how did it happen?" asked Jo. "I don't understand. What did we do?"

No one knew. Jo stopped suddenly. There was something odd about the tracks on the ground.

What has Jo seen?

Scraps of Paper

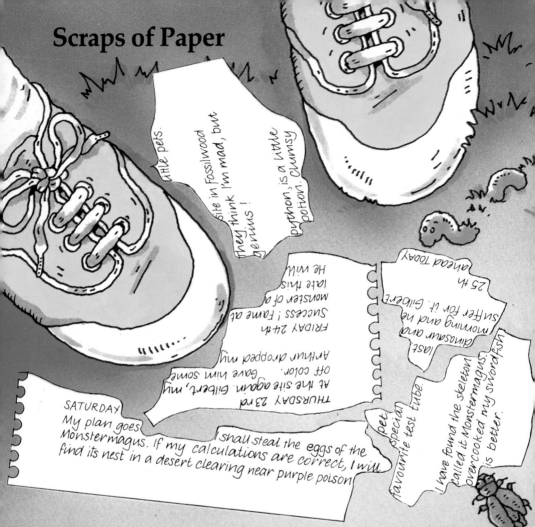

Further on in the jungle, Freddie noticed some torn-up scraps of paper lying in the grass. Each one was covered in black, spidery writing. He picked them up and pieced them together like a jigsaw puzzle.

"It's a page from somebody's diary," Jo exclaimed.

"And whoever wrote it is here with us now," added Zack, looking at the bottom of the page. "The last date is August 25th. That's today."

Piece together the scraps of paper to find out what is written in the diary.

Hands Up

Freddie was worried. Whoever wrote the diary had some very weird ideas.

"I think we should watch out," he said.

"So you should," answered a sinister voice. "Hands up!"

They looked up – straight into the barrel of a shot gun. At the other end was a white-haired man wearing a bow tie.

"What are you doing here?" demanded the man. "That's MY diary and you've walked through MY time door."

Then he shouted at the miserable-looking boy standing beside him. Jo gasped in surprise. It was Arthur, star of the school science club.

"It's all your fault Arthur," yelled the man. "Tie these spies up at once."

Arthur looked even more miserable, but he did as he was told. Jo tried to speak to him, but he wouldn't look at her.

The man prodded Freddie in the back with the barrel of his gun and ordered them to move. He marched them along at break-neck speed, deeper and deeper into the thick, tropical jungle. Curious eyes stared out at them from the undergrowth.

Large drops of rain splashed down and mud squelched under their feet. But still they walked on . . . and on.

Zack glanced back at the man. His face was very familiar. He was sure he had seen him before.

Do you know who the man is? What is his name?

19

Prisoners Underground

The Professor stopped suddenly. Ahead lay a large hole in the ground.

"Stop!" barked the Professor. "This is the end of the road for you three meddlesome brats."

He dragged Zack by the scruff of his neck and pushed him down into the hole. Then he grabbed Jo.

"Down you go," he sneered. "You should make very interesting fossils."

When Freddie's turn came something strange happened. The Professor turned away for a split second and Arthur thrust a scrap of paper into his hand. But there was no time to look at it. Freddie skidded down the hole and along a dark, wet tunnel. Then he felt himself falling down and down into the darkness.

He landed on a mound of soft earth, next to Zack and Jo. They were sitting in a shadowy, underground cave. It was cold, dark and wet. What were they going to do?

Freddie unfolded Arthur's note. He wanted to help them! But first they had to find a way out of the cave. Zack tried climbing up to the tunnel, but he was pushed back by a stream of water pouring into the cave. There was a hole in the roof, but it was too high to reach.

By now, the tunnel stream had become a torrent and water was splashing around their ankles . . . and their knees. They had to find a way out FAST or they would drown.

In a flash of inspiration, Freddie realized he had something that would save their lives and help them to escape from the cave.

How can they escape?

On the Trail

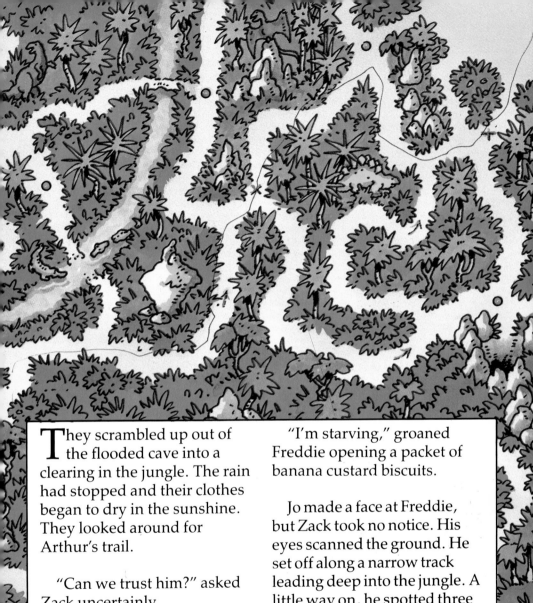

They scrambled up out of the flooded cave into a clearing in the jungle. The rain had stopped and their clothes began to dry in the sunshine. They looked around for Arthur's trail.

"Can we trust him?" asked Zack uncertainly.

They had no choice. Arthur was the only one who could lead them to the Professor. And without the Professor, there was no chance of getting home.

"I'm starving," groaned Freddie opening a packet of banana custard biscuits.

Jo made a face at Freddie, but Zack took no notice. His eyes scanned the ground. He set off along a narrow track leading deep into the jungle. A little way on, he spotted three twigs in the shape of an arrow. It was the start of Arthur's trail.

Can you follow Arthur's trail through the jungle?

Flying Monsters

At the edge of the jungle, they heard a loud wooshing noise. All around, the trees began to rustle. They looked up and saw an enormous flying dinosaur.

"It's a Pteranodon," said Freddie in a know-all voice.

The Pteranodon swooped down and seized Jo and Freddie in its sharp claws. Then it opened its beak and grabbed Zack by his collar. It soared above the jungle, away from the trail, and dropped them on a high rocky crag.

"I think we're next on the menu," Zack gulped.

But just as the dinosaur opened its giant beak, a shadow fell across the rock. An even bigger monster appeared in the sky flying towards them.

"It's a Quetzalcoatlus!" shrieked Freddie.

It dived, screeching, at the Pteranodon and the two monsters flew into battle. Jo crossed her fingers and shut her eyes tight . . .

When she opened them again, the monsters had gone. They were safe, but they had lost Arthur's trail. How would they find the Professor and the Monstermagus nest now?

Zack had an idea. He pulled out his pocket compass. North was directly behind him.

Where is the nest?

85

A Dangerous Descent

First they had to climb down the mountain. The ground seemed a very long way off. Below them was a series of strange pillar rocks.

"We can jump from one rock to the next and climb over the tree," said Freddie. "But there are some terrible things in the way."

There were poisonous snakes and vapour pools, dangerous rubble and spiky bushes, a bubbling stream of red-hot lava . . . and dinosaurs.

"Follow me," said Zack leaping onto the first pillar.

Can you find a safe route down the rockface, dodging all the obstacles?

Journey through the Jungle

Keeping the blue-capped volcano in sight, they headed off through the unknown jungle. All around, they could hear strange noises and rustlings. They stopped abruptly. Straight ahead, was a dinosaur the size of an elephant.

"It's an Allosaurus," said Freddie, cheerfully. "Where's my camera? Imagine him next to Dad in my photo album."

Neither Zack nor Jo wanted to hang about taking photos. They turned and dashed away. Freddie followed . . . and so did the Allosaurus.

They ran at full pelt until they were ready to drop, but the dinosaur showed no signs of slowing up. Suddenly Zack stopped under a tall tree. He jumped up, grabbed a sturdy branch and hauled himself up. Jo and Freddie did the same.

Yoa urv ern yeat rhn eesd. Ton'w torra ybout thm eonstermagut. Shp erofessor'd sarw tilp lui tt ts oleef poo rnh eouy. Roc uaf nint dht eimd eooro st nhp erofessor't simc ehari - tt'a so nlt, dorr nolo lp fapet riew dito hnr eer dibbon.

Perched up high among the leaves, they felt safe. The Allosaurus paused below them and looked up. It snarled and gnashed its teeth, but it couldn't reach them.

At last it walked on. They waited until it was out of sight before climbing back down to the ground. Then Jo spotted the crumpled piece of paper pinned to a tree trunk.

"We must be back on Arthur's trail," she cried excitedly.

Jo unpinned the paper and groaned. The message was in code.

"I can't work it out at all," she said. "You two have a look."

Can you decode Arthur's message?

At the Nest

They crept on. It wasn't far now. The clearing lay straight ahead and in the distance, they could see the steaming poison pools.

All of a sudden, Zack saw the Professor. He was standing in a hollow beside eight large, white eggs. Behind him lay an enormous, sleeping dinosaur. It was the Monstermagus.

They ducked behind a boulder and watched the Professor lift the eggs out of the nest. He examined them one by one.

"He's stealing the eggs," gasped Freddie. "We've got to stop him."

But there was nothing they could do. The Professor laid the eggs in a large metal chest, closed the lid and tapped some buttons on the top. Then he called to Arthur and marched off briskly towards the blue-capped volcano carrying only a camera and tripod.

"It's our big chance," said Zack. "Quickly! Let's take the eggs."

If they replaced the eggs with stones, the Professor would never know they were gone. But there was one problem. The box was locked.

"It's a combination lock," said Jo, looking at the buttons on the lid. "You press certain buttons in a special order to unlock it."

Some buttons were numbered, others were blank. Which ones should they press?

Then Freddie noticed a scrap of paper lying beside the metal chest. There was a list of confusing instructions written on it.

"These might help," he said, reading the first one aloud.

Which buttons should they press to open the box? You will need to find the missing numbers first.

Each row and diagonal adds up to 15.

The buttons are numbered 1 to 9.

Press the evens to open and the odds to close, in ascending order.

The Professor's Papers

Freddie carefully lifted the eggs out of the chest and Zack carried them back to the nest. The Monstermagus was still sleeping peacefully. Jo filled the chest with stones and locked it again.

"Now we've got to find the Professor's time chart," she said.

Freddie started emptying the Professor's bags onto the ground. There were hundreds of maps and papers. But which one was the time chart? They had to find it fast. The Professor could return at any moment.

Can you find the time chart?

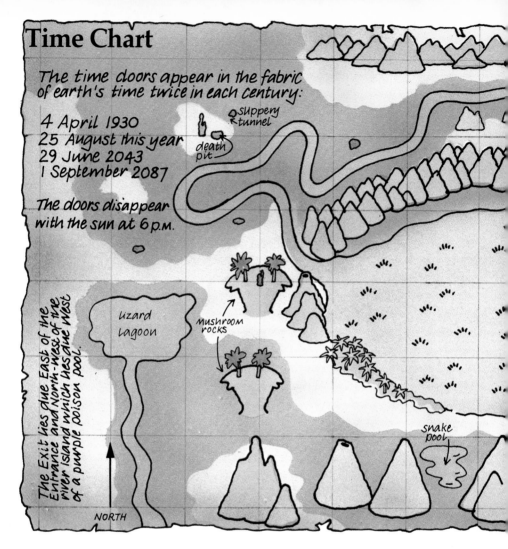

Time Chart

The time doors appear in the fabric of earth's time twice in each century:

4 April 1930
25 August this year
29 June 2043
1 September 2087

The doors disappear with the sun at 6 p.m.

slippery tunnel

death pit

The Exit lies due East of the Entrance and North-West of the river island which lies due West of a purple poison pool.

lizard lagoon

mushroom rocks

snake pool

NORTH

Zack untied the red ribbon and carefully unrolled the tattered, old chart. He spread it out on the ground in front of them.

"It's a map of the whole area," Jo exclaimed. "The Professor must have been here before."

Zack, Jo and Freddie stared blankly at the map. They were stumped. The nest was marked with an arrow. But where was the time door? It wasn't shown anywhere.

"This is hopeless," Freddie wailed. "We'll never find our way home."

There are two time doors, an Entrance and an Exit. Both appear as a hole through which the past or future can be seen.

mushroom rock

pillar rocks

lava pool

crocodile swamp

swamp island

river islands

purple poison pools

blue-capped volcano

nest

The Entrance lies due East of the death pit and North-East of the tree stump on the mushroom rock.

Jo was about to agree when she started reading the strange, spidery notes scrawled at the sides of the map.

"I think these are clues," she explained, pointing at the notes. "If we work out the compass bearings, we can find the time door."

Jo studied the map while Zack and Freddie kept watch.

"I've found it," Jo said.

. . . Just in time. The Professor was returning. Quickly, they dived for cover.

Can you find the time door?

Crocodile Swamp

The Professor stared in horror at the mess. Papers and maps lay everywhere.

"Run for it," Zack yelled, sprinting towards the jungle.

Too late. The Professor spotted them at once and started off in hot pursuit.

Zack, Jo and Freddie ran on and on as fast as they could, until they came to the edge of a vast, steamy swamp.

"We've got to cross this swamp," said Zack. "It's the quickest way to the time door."

"We can use that hollow tree trunk as a canoe," said a voice.

It was Arthur! He had escaped from the Professor. Jo and Freddie scrambled into the trunk, as Zack and Arthur pushed them out into the swamp. But what could they use as paddles?

"We can't use our hands," said Arthur. "Look at those crocodiles!"

He was right. Then Jo realized she and Zack both had something they could use.

What can they use as paddles?

Freddie and the Monstermagus

At the other side, the swamp was surrounded by a wall of steep mountains and volcanoes. There was only one way through – a narrow, muddy pass at the foot of a smoking volcano. A stream of red-hot lava was starting to pour down the side of the volcano towards the pass.

They dashed to the pass, ran under a rocky ledge and on to safety. But where was Freddie? They looked back. He was still a long way off, paddling in the water. And there behind him was . . . a huge Monstermagus.

"What can we do? What's going to happen?" wailed Jo.

Ledge

"It's obvious," said Arthur, tapping his calculator keys.

Zack and Jo looked blank, so Arthur explained.

"The lava is heading for that ledge. Freddie has to run eight yards to pass under its midpoint and he does 100 yards in 25 seconds."

"The lava flows two yards in a second. It's 18 feet above the ledge which is 51 feet from the ground. The Monstermagus is 16 yards behind Freddie, runs six yards a second and we already know how tall it is."

Can you work out what happens?

Looking for the Time Door

They clambered on up through the pass until they came out into open ground. They could see jungle just a little way ahead. The time door was here somewhere . . .

Freddie stopped shaking and began grumbling.

"I was nearly eaten and it's all your fault, Zack," he muttered. "This expedition was your idea. I was quite happy being bored at home."

But no one was taking any notice. They were running out of time.

Zack unrolled the Professor's chart. There were now only minutes left before the time door disappeared. They HAD to find it.

"We're in the right place," said Zack. "But where's the door?"

"We have to look for it," said Arthur. "It should be easy to see."

They paced up and down searching. Suddenly they spotted it!

Where is the time door?

The Footprint Fossil

Back in their own time, it was hard to believe it had ever happened. Fossilwood Forest was as dark and gloomy as ever and even the Professor looked less crazy.

From behind a bush, they watched as the Professor struggled through the forest with his precious chest. What would he do when he realized it was full of stones? What would he say when he discovered Arthur had taken the film out of his camera?

The next day, they took the Monstermagus claw and a few prehistoric shells to the museum. The first thing they saw was the famous footprints fossil. They gazed at the small human shoeprint.

"You know who made it don't you?" Jo laughed.

"No one would believe us if we tried to explain!" said Zack.

Do you know who made the fossil footprint?

Clues

Pages 6-7
You can see what the claw looks like in Zack's newspaper on page 5.

Pages 8-9
This is easy. First follow Zack's route to find out where it takes them. Then follow Jo's and Freddie's routes in turn.

Pages 10-11
Freddie's dinosaur book on pages 12 and 13 makes this easy.

Pages 14-15
Work out which are Zack, Jo and Freddie's footprints. Are there any others?

Pages 16-17
Trace each piece of paper, or photocopy the page and cut out the pieces. Match them up and stick them together to read the diary.

Pages 18-19
Look back at Zack's newspaper on page 5.

Pages 20-21
What does Freddie have with him? Look at pages 6 and 7.

Pages 22-23
You don't need a clue for this. Use your eyes.

Pages 24-25
Arthur's note on page 19 and Professor Crank-Pott's diary on pages 16 and 17 should give you some hints.

Pages 26-27
This is easy. They can jump from pillar to pillar and climb over the tree.

Pages 28-29
Try exchanging the last letter of the first word with the first letter of the next word.

Pages 30-31
Find the missing numbers first. Ascending means going up.

Pages 32-33
Arthur's note on page 29 describes the time chart.

Pages 34-35
Find the time door entrance first. Remember the points of the compass:

Pages 36-37
What equipment do both Zack and Jo have? Look at pages 6 and 7.

Pages 38-39
Use Arthur's figures to work out how long it will take Freddie, the Monstermagus and the lava to pass the ledge.

Pages 40-41
Can you spot anything unusual in the picture?

Page 42
Look back through the book at everyone's shoeprints.

Answers

Pages 6-7

Here is the Monstermagus claw.

Pages 8-9

This map shows each person's route. Freddie's is the only correct one. Zack's route takes them to the Wild Woods.

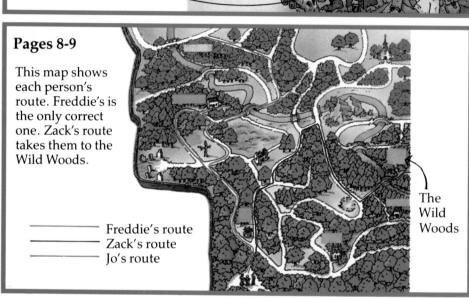

——————— Freddie's route
——————— Zack's route
——————— Jo's route

The Wild Woods

Pages 10-11

Here you can see which dinosaurs eat meat and which eat plants.

Meat-eaters

Plant-eaters

Probably a plant-eating Diplodocus

Meat-eater

Meat-eater

Plant-eaters

Meat-eater

Meat-eaters

Plant-eater

44

Pages 14-15

Jo has seen five different sets of shoeprints. This means two other people have also travelled backwards in time.

These footprints do not belong to Zack, Jo or Freddie.

Freddie's footprint

Zack's footprint

Jo's footprint

Pages 16-17

This is the page from the diary, when the pieces are put together.

AUGUST
MONDAY 20th
All the figures work. At long last I've found the secret of the time door again. Recruited a boy called Arthur as my assistant. He's brilliant at sums, but I don't like children at all.

TUESDAY 21st
Making plans. The time door appears on Saturday. I shall travel back 150 million years and steal some dinosaur eggs. Then I shall bring them home and hatch them I shall cause chaos in the modern world with my little pets.

WEDNESDAY 22nd
Spent the day digging at the dinosaur site in Fossilwood Forest with a lot of silly experts. They think I'm mad, but I'll prove them wrong – I'm a genius!

THURSDAY 23rd
At the site again Gilbert, my pet python, is a little off color   Gave him some special potion. Clumsy Arthur dropped my favourite test tube.

FRIDAY 24th
Success! Fame at last. I have found the skeleton of a real monster of a dinosaur and called it Monstermagus. Arthur was late this morning and he overcooked my swordfish steak. He will suffer for it. Gilbert is better.

SATURDAY 25th
My plan goes ahead TODAY. I shall steal the eggs of the Monstermagus. If my calculations are correct, I will find its nest in a desert clearing near purple poison pools.

Pages 18-19

The man is Professor Crank-Pott. Zack recognizes him from the newspaper photo on page 5, shown below.

Pages 20-21

Freddie has an inflatable air cushion (see pages 6 and 7). They can blow it up and cling on to it. This will keep them afloat as the cave floods. When the water reaches the roof, they can scramble out of the hole at the top.

Pages 22-23

Arthur's trail is marked here in black.

Pages 24-25

The nest is behind this volcano. Arthur's note on page 21 says the nest is South of a blue-capped volcano, South of the swamp. The Professor's diary on pages 16 and 17 says it is in a desert clearing near purple poison pools.

South is directly ahead of Zack.

Pages 26-27

The route down the rocky pillars is marked in black.

They climb over this tree.

Pages 28-29

The message is decoded by swapping the last letter of every word with the first letter of the next.

You are very near the nest. Don't worry about the Monstermagus. The Professor's dart will put it to sleep for one hour. You can find the time doors on the Professor's time chart – it's an old, torn roll of paper tied with one red ribbon.

Pages 30-31

Here is the box with the missing numbers added. The buttons marked 2, 4, 6 and 8 will open the lock.

Pages 32-33

This is the only one of the papers that fits Arthur's description on page 29.

Pages 34-35

The compass bearings pinpoint the time doors, marked below.

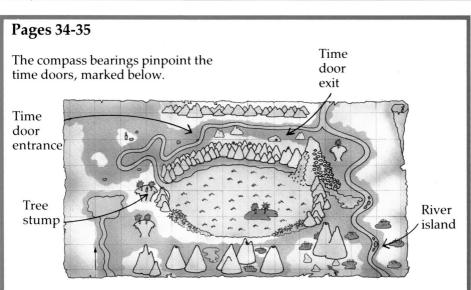

Time door exit

Time door entrance

Tree stump

River island

Pages 36-37

Zack and Jo both have spades which they can use as paddles.

Pages 38-39

Freddie runs four yards a second so he will pass under the ledge in two seconds' time. The lava will reach the ledge, way above him, in three seconds' time, so Freddie is safe.

The Monstermagus will pass under the ledge in four seconds' time. At this point, the lava will be 45 feet from the ground which means it will hit the Monstermagus on the head. The Monstermagus is 45 feet tall (see Zack's newspaper on page 5).

Pages 40-41

Here is the time door.

Through it, you can see St Elmo's Church, shown in the map on pages 8 and 9.

Page 42

Freddie is the only one whose footprint matches the fossil print. The print was made in the soft mud when Freddie was running away from Monstermagus. The volcanic lava preserved his and the dinosaur's footprints, as well as the dinosaur's skeleton. They eventually became fossils (see pages 12 and 13).

The human fossil footprint.

Freddie's footprint.

THE INTERGALACTIC BUS TRIP

Martin Oliver

Illustrated by
Brenda Haw and Martin Newton

Designed by
Patrick Knowles and Kim Blundell

Contents

About this Story

The Intergalactic Bus Trip is an action-packed adventure that takes you on an out-of-this-world journey, through alien planets, to the far reaches of unknown space.

Along the way, there are lots of fun puzzles and tricky problems to solve. Find the answers to these before going on to the next episode in the story.

Look at the pictures carefully and watch out for vital clues and information. Sometimes you will need to flick back through the story to help you find an answer.

There are extra clues on page 91 and you can check your answers on pages 92 to 96.

Just turn the page to begin the adventure...

The Computer Game

Tom and Izzy were playing a record-breaking game of 'Robot Raiders'. The score was 2,325,998 to 2,325,999 and Tom was winning. He had never got this far before. In fact, no one had ever got this far before.

Tom's spaceship dodged and weaved through a hail of missiles and exploding bombs. He took careful aim and pressed the trigger.

My score's been wiped out!

Sssh. Look at the computer.

CLICK. They were plunged into darkness and a strange humming sound filled the room. The computer buzzed and whirred.

Tom yelled at the computer, but Izzy took no notice. She was staring at the screen in surprise. It began to glow an eerie green, as a series of strange symbols appeared.

"I think it's some sort of message," said Izzy, studying the screen. "But I'm not sure how to read it."

"Forget it," said Tom, crossly. "The computer must be broken."

Can you read the message?

On to the Bus

A few days later, Tom and Izzy were late for the cinema. As they ran down the road, a Number Nine bus drew up beside them.

"Come on. Let's take the bus," Izzy shouted, jumping aboard.

"Two tickets please," said Tom, looking at the driver in surprise.

Izzy walked on down the bus towards some empty seats at the back.

The doors slammed shut. As Izzy looked around , she spotted several very odd things . . . this was not a normal bus.

How many odd things can you see?

Lift-Off

Before Izzy could say anything, there was a loud bang and the bus lurched forwards. Tom went flying as the bus moved faster and faster. It hurtled along the High Street and swerved round a corner shop.

Passengers and papers flew everywhere. Tom gazed out of the window in disbelief as the bus left the ground and soared into the air. Houses and trees disappeared below as the bus roared onwards and upwards through the clouds.

Izzy hung on to her seat and watched in amazement as Tom floated up. What was happening? Tom drifted past her and bumped gently against the window. He stared out in horror, beginning to feel very ill. Where were they going?

What they needed was a map. As Tom slumped down beside her, Izzy remembered seeing one, but where was it? She racked her brains. Just then she felt a tap on her shoulder . . .

Can you find the bus map?

Roger the Martian

A large eye blinked at Izzy. The eye was attached to a long, wobbly antenna and the antenna was connected to a smiling, green thing.

"Perhaps I can help," said the thing, pulling the bus map out of his pocket.

Izzy gawped in amazement. Who was this strange creature?

"My name is Roger," he said. "I'm on my way to Zenos, but I come from Mars."

"You speak very good English," Izzy exclaimed.

"Of course," replied the Martian. "I went to Earth on a school trip last year."

Izzy asked Roger if he knew how to get back to Earth. But Roger looked puzzled and scratched his head.

"I think you should get off at the next stop," he said, studying the map.

What is the next stop?

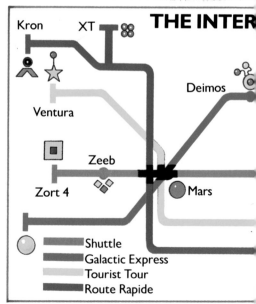

THE INTER

Kron XT

Ventura

Zeeb

Zort 4

Deimos

Mars

Shuttle
Galactic Express
Tourist Tour
Route Rapide

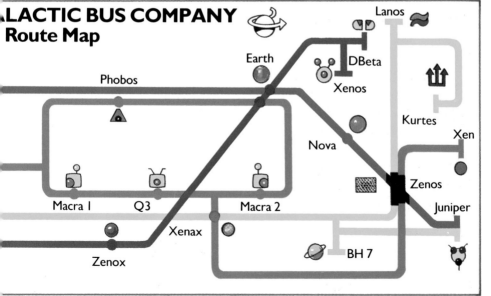

LACTIC BUS COMPANY
Route Map

Lanos

Earth

DBeta

Phobos

Xenos

Kurtes

Xen

Nova

Zenos

Macra 1   Q3   Macra 2

Juniper

Xenax

Zenox

BH 7

The Arrival Processing Plant

As the droid driver announced the next stop, the bus began to orbit a pink planet. It hovered over the landing zone and started its descent. Izzy wondered if she would ever see home again.

The bus bounced on to the cosmic concrete. It screeched to a halt and there was a mad scramble as all the other passengers rushed off the bus.

"Wh... where are we?" Tom stammered, opening his eyes.

"We're on Nova," replied Roger, heading towards the door. "Follow me. My friend Norman lives here. He's bound to know how to get you on the next Earth-bound bus."

Tom and Izzy jumped off the bus and saw eleven doors ahead of them.

"We must find a door that we can all go through, or we'll lose each other," said Roger.

Which door can they go through?

In Nova New Town

Roger whisked them through the Processing Plant and out into Nova New Town. He fumbled in his voluminous pockets and pulled out a very grubby school photograph.

"There's Norman," said Roger. "He's sitting to my left, third from the right, behind the blue blob."

At the bottom, Norman had scribbled his address. Roger looked up and groaned. All the buildings looked the same to him. How would they ever find Norman?

"I know," said Izzy, suddenly. "Follow me."

Can you identify Norman? Where does he live?

Flat 3, floor 14, Megalith Tower (the flat fronted blue building with a flat roof — very close to the monorail).

63

Action Replay

Izzy dashed ahead. But three minutes, two left turns and one dead-end later, she noticed that Tom and Roger were no longer following.

Retracing her steps, she turned a corner and gasped. Roger was lying on the ground. He had turned a very funny shade of turquoise.

"Roger, are you O.K?" she asked. "You don't look well."

"I'm fine," groaned Roger. "Just a bit off colour. But Tom..."

Roger wasn't sure what had happened to Tom. He struggled to his feet, looking very unsteady.

"My photographic memory might help," he said. "But it's a bit confused."

Izzy watched in amazement as Roger projected a series of photographs into the air. If she could put them into order, she would be able to find out what had happened to Tom.

Can you work out what happened to Tom?

Norman the Novan

Roger and Izzy looked at each other, their minds racing. Why had the aliens snatched Tom? Where were they taking him? And who were they?

Roger directed his antennae at the pink Novan sky.

"I can see the kidnappers' ship," he shouted. "Quick. We must get back to the bus and follow them."

They set off through the streets, turned left and THUD. They collided with a small, round, bouncy creature.

High-Fliers come to
THE JET-SET CLUB

NATTY NOVAN KNITWEAR

Out to lunch. Back 92.95

SALE
100% Reductions

"Norman!" exclaimed Roger. "We've been looking for you. This is my new Earth-thing friend..."

"Yes I know. Hello Izzy," said Norman, waggling his outsize ears proudly. "I overheard. I think I can help you by zeroing in on the kidnappers' frequency."

Norman frowned. His orange hair stood on end and his ears buzzed as he relayed a long series of numbers. What did they mean? Was it some sort of coded message?

Can you decode the message? Who has kidnapped Tom and where is he being taken?

Back on the Bus

THE SHOOTING STAR SNACK BAR

Roger kept one eye trained on the kidnappers' ship, as he and Izzy followed Norman back to the bus. Puffing and panting they clambered aboard.

"I'll drive," wheezed Roger, brandishing a piece of yellow plastic. "Here's my universal driving licence. Hang on tight. We'll soon get Tom back from those Rogue Robots."

The bus taxied into the take-off area. Roger pressed the power pedal and they began to accelerate. Izzy was just about to secure the doors when, to her surprise, she saw Tom running towards the bus.

"Abort take-off," shouted Roger as he spotted the advancing figure.

Izzy stared hard at Tom for a moment. All of a sudden, she hit the automatic door-locking button.

"Take off!" she yelled. "It's a trick."

Is she right?

On the Vapour Trail

Roger checked the instruments again and flicked the lift-off lever. Within seconds they were space-borne, tracking the kidnappers' route with the help of Norman's sonic ear sensors. But just as they rounded a deserted, green planet, Norman's ears went floppy.

"The signal's faded," he cried. "I've lost track of the Robots' ship."

Roger scanned the sky with his telescopic eye. All he could see was a tangled web of vapour trails around Interstellar Junction 15. Then Izzy had a brain wave.

"Let's follow the kidnappers' vapour trail," she said.

Can you follow the vapour trail?

Collision Course

The bus wove its way through the tangled trails out into open space. It whizzed through the cosmos, past satellites and stars until, at last, the Robots' ship was in sight.

Suddenly Roger saw a meteor hurtling towards the bus. He slammed on the brakes but it was too late. They were on a collision course. Izzy dived for cover...

Minutes later, she crawled out from under her seat feeling dazed. Roger was looking at the engine and Norman was rummaging in the repair kit.

"What happened?" asked Izzy, peering at the engine.

"We crash-parked on this service satellite," replied Norman. "The engine's broken."

"Then we must fix it," said Izzy, picking up a spanner.

Can you repair the engine?

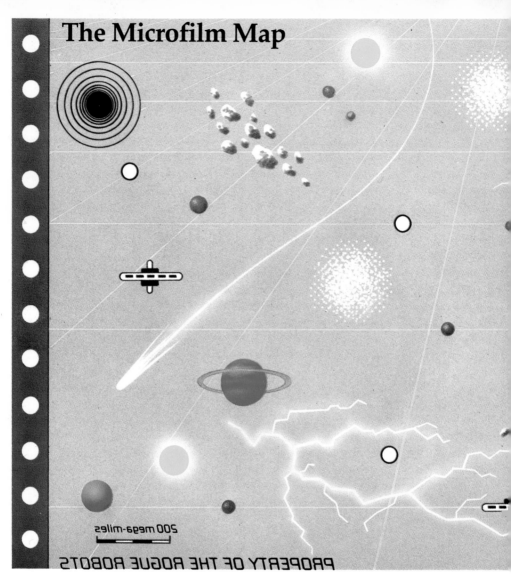

The Microfilm Map

200 mega-miles

PROPERTY OF THE ROGUE ROBOTS

Roger pressed the starter switch. The engine spluttered into life and the bus roared off. Norman and Roger scanned the stratosphere with their eyes and ears open wide, but the kidnappers had vanished without trace.

"It's hopeless," snuffled Izzy. "We'll never find Tom."

Roger parked the bus on the edge of a small sun. He dug into his pockets for a handkerchief. Out fell a tiny square of microfilm.

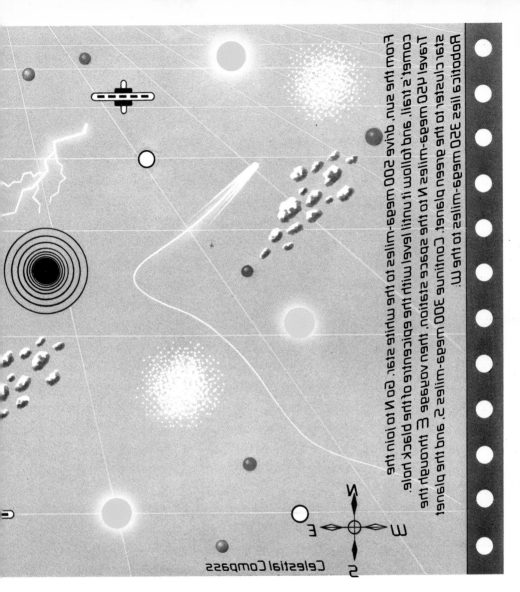

Robotica lies 350 mega-miles to the W. Travel 450 mega-miles N to the green planet. Continue 300 mega-miles S and 200 mega-miles E through the comet's tail, follow it until the white star, dive 500 mega-miles to the white star. Go to join the space station, then voyage E through the black hole, space level fit it until the white star, dive 500 mega-miles to the blue planet.

Celestial Compass

   "I'd forgotten about this," he said, holding it up to the light. "I found it on the ground when Tom disappeared."

   "It's a microfilm map," Izzy exclaimed. "And it belongs to the Rogue Robots."

   Then she saw some strange writing on one side of the map. If only she could decipher it, she was sure it would lead them to the Robots' Planet.

Where is the bus?
What is the route to Robotica?

Speeding on the Skyway

Roger started up the bus again and set off towards Robotica. They drove on and on, through mega-mile after mega-mile of empty space until they reached the start of the South Orbital Skyway. The bus slowed down and Izzy looked at the time read-out on the Skyway Signpost in dismay.

Time was running out. The Robots would reach their base in 26 micro-minutes and the bus was a long way behind. Izzy hoped the read-out might be wrong. But it wasn't. The green dashboard clock showed the same time and the dashboard clock was never wrong. Roger hit the boost button.

Cosmic time check at 93:15. Observation bulletin to all patrols. One red bus entering South Orbital Skyway.

XR7 EXIT : 900 mega-miles
PLUTON EXIT : 855 mega-miles

MAX. SPEED 60 mega-miles per micro-minute

MAX. SPEED 55 mega-miles per micro-minute

MAX. SPEED 75 mega-miles per micro-minute

macro-hours > 93:15 < micro-minutes

The bus rocketed down the skyway. As they passed the Pluton exit, they saw a flashing light and screeched to a halt in front of a grim-looking skyway patrolman.

"You're booked," he growled. "You were speeding on the skyway."

Roger didn't know what to say. After all, he had been driving very fast . . .

"No we weren't," cried Izzy. "And I can prove it."

Was the bus speeding on the skyway?

Searching for the Base

695 mega-miles further on, the planet Robotica was in sight. The bus slowed down and Roger put the controls onto auto-orbit. He stuck his antennae out of the window and scanned the alien landscape below. There was no sign of Tom or the Robots. Where was the base?

Just then, Norman's ears began to buzz. He pointed down to the planet surface.

"I'm picking up high-frequency signals," he explained.

"Where are they coming from?" asked Izzy, excitedly.

Norman pin-pointed seven landmarks: the sapphire stone, the space-ship wreck, the tower roof, the aerial mast, the blue bridge, the ventilation shaft and the red rock.

"They make a pattern," said Izzy, drawing imaginary lines between the signals. "Perhaps they will lead us to the base."

Where is the Robots' base?

Crash, bang, bump. Roger landed the bus. They scrambled into space suits and floated out of the door.

The planet was covered in a thick, invisible gas. Drifting was easy, but getting anywhere was much more tricky.

Roger and Norman swam ahead towards a door in the green cliff. It was locked.

Norman pointed to the panel of numbered buttons beside the door. The only way to open it was to tap in a special, secret number sequence.

A sudden gust of gas knocked over a dustbin beside the door. Roger snatched at the scraps of floating space debris. Numbers were scribbled on them.

"I think they make a sequence," said Roger, enlarging the scraps with his right eye. "We must fit them together to find out."

Some of the pieces were missing which left gaps in the sequence. But it wasn't hard to work out the missing numbers.

Izzy paddled up to the door and punched the sequence onto the numbered keys. Very slowly, the door slid open.

What are the missing numbers?

Inside the Base

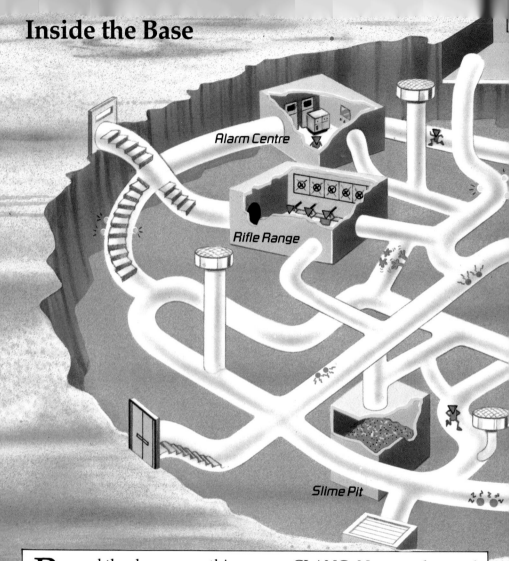

Alarm Centre

Rifle Range

Slime Pit

Beyond the door, everything was dark. Izzy hoped that she was looking braver than she felt as she entered the base.

"We must be quiet," Roger whispered. "The Rogue Robots will have sound sensors hidden all over the place."

CLANG. Norman dropped his helmet. They stopped still and held their breath, waiting for an alarm to ring. But all they could hear was the helmet bouncing down some steps.

"Whoops," said Norman and scuttled after his helmet.

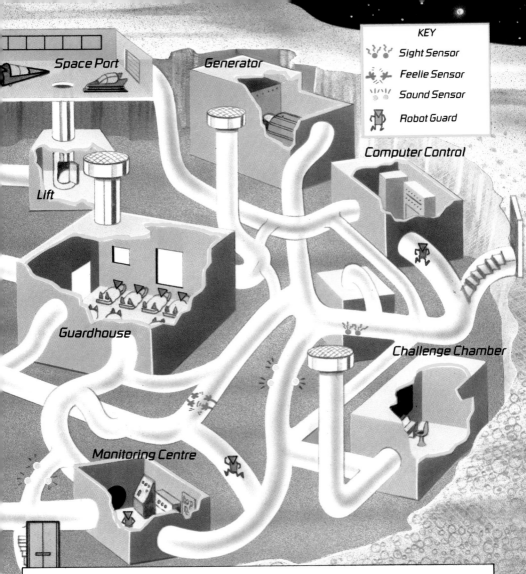

Space Port

Generator

Computer Control

Lift

Guardhouse

Challenge Chamber

Monitoring Centre

   Roger and Izzy followed on tiptoes, down the steps and straight on to a junction. Here they turned left and felt a cool, gassy breeze from a ventilation shaft on their right. They followed the passage as it bent round in a U shape, ignoring the turning to the left.

   The passage bent to the left and then to the right where it forked in two. In the middle of the two forks, Izzy spotted a map of the base. Now they could work out how to get to Tom.

Where are they and how can they reach Tom?

The Key to the Challenge Chamber

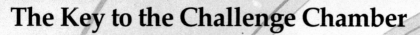

Ahead lay the locked door of the Challenge Chamber. Norman acted as listen-out, while Roger examined the lock.

"We need a key like this," said Roger, projecting the image of a key shape.

Izzy saw a bunch of keys hanging on the wall. One of them was bound to fit the lock. She reached up and picked them off the hook . . .

"No!" yelled Roger.

Too late! Sirens wailed and red lights flashed as Izzy fumbled with the keys.

"Hurry up," yelled Norman. "I can hear a troop of Robots and they're coming this way."

Which key will open the door to the Challenge Chamber?

85

Robot Raiders

They sprinted through the open door as the Rogue Robots started firing their stun guns. Izzy slammed the door shut and ran towards Tom. He was strapped to a chair in front of a giant 'Robot Raiders' screen.

"What are you doing playing computer games?" gasped Izzy.

"I'm not," gulped Tom. "It's for real this time. If I lose, the Robots will destroy us."

Roger and Norman looked puzzled, so Izzy explained.

"Tom has to isolate each of the enemy rockets," she said. "But he only has three defence discs left to fire."

"What's a defence disc?" asked Norman, feeling confused.

"It's a green circle, exactly like the one on the screen," Tom explained.

All of a sudden, a menacing metallic voice rang out through the chamber.

"No one can beat the Rogue Robots," snarled the voice. "You were fools to challenge us. Now you will die. There is no way out."

"That's what you think," yelled Izzy, grabbing the controls from Tom's hand.

Can you beat the computer?

Laser Maze

The lights began to flicker and the screen went blank as the metallic voice echoed through the chamber.

"You may think you've beaten us, but we shall win in the end. This planet is programmed to self-destruct and even if you leave it in time, you will never escape the laser maze."

They didn't wait to hear any more. Roger untied Tom and they all sprinted out of the chamber, back along smoke-filled corridors, out of the base and onto the bus.

Roger set the controls for vertical take off and pressed the hyperspace switch. The bus rocketed up and away only seconds before the planet exploded into a ball of fire.

Izzy glanced at the radar screen. The exploding planet was surrounded by a maze of lethal laser rays. They had to find a way through it to escape the blast . . . and quickly.

Can you find a way through the maze to safety?

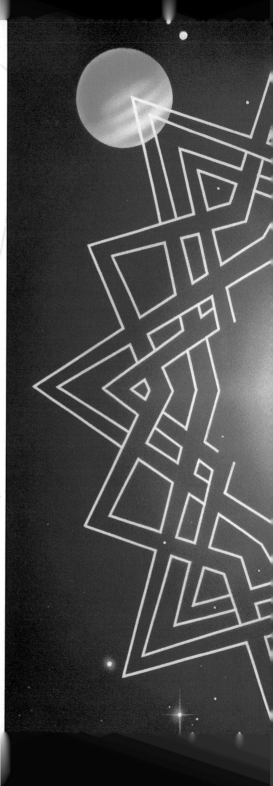

Back to Earth

And that was the last thing Tom and Izzy could remember. When they next opened their eyes, they were back in the High Street. They stumbled off the bus feeling very confused. Had their adventure really happened, or was it all a dream?

"Whatever happened to Roger and Norman?" asked Tom.

Izzy looked back at the bus and up and down the High Street. There was no sign of them anywhere. Or was there?

What do you think?

Clues

Pages 52-53

Hold the page in front of a mirror.

Pages 54-55

This is easy. Use your eyes.

Pages 56-57

Look carefully at each picture.

Pages 58-59

Where is the bus going? Where did Tom, Izzy and Roger get on?

Pages 60-61

Remember they are not from Nova.

Pages 62-63

Which is Roger's right in the photograph? Only one building matches Norman's description.

Pages 64-65

This is easy.

Pages 66-67

1=A, 26=Z. You will need to add punctuation marks.

Pages 68-69

Look at the other pictures of Tom.

Pages 70-71

You don't need a clue for this.

Pages 72-73

Which parts of the engine are broken? Are any parts missing?

Pages 74-75

The map is shown back to front. Use a mirror to read the instructions.

Pages 76-77

Which is the dashboard clock? To work out the speed of the bus, divide the distance it travelled by the time it took.

Pages 78-79

Join up the signal landmarks. What pattern do they make?

Pages 80-81

Piece the scraps together. The numbers don't increase by the same amount each time.

Pages 82-83

The Robots' message on page 67 tells you where to find Tom.

Pages 84-85

Look at the keys and the lock carefully.

Pages 86-87

The first defence disc goes here.

Pages 88-89

There are two entrances and exits.

Page 90

Keep your eyes and ears open.

Answers

Pages 52-53

The message is written back to front and upside down. To read it, turn the page the other way up and hold it in front of a mirror. This is what it says:

Who has dared challenge the Rogue Robots at their own game? Beware Earth-thing, soon you will be playing for your life. We shall strike when you least expect it.

Pages 54-55

Here you can see what Izzy spotted.

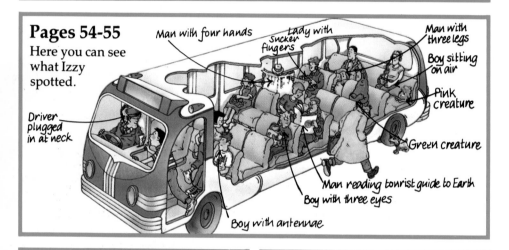

Man with four hands

Lady with sucker fingers

Man with three legs

Boy sitting on air

Pink creature

Driver plugged in at neck

Green creature

Man reading tourist guide to Earth

Boy with three eyes

Boy with antennae

Pages 56-57

Here is the bus map.

Pages 58-59

The last stop, where Tom and Izzy boarded the bus, was Earth. Roger is travelling from Mars to Zenos and the bus is going to Juniper. The only line that stops at all these places is the Galactic Express. The next stop is Nova.

Pages 60-61

The only door they can all go through is the one labelled "Two-Eyed Aliens".

Pages 62-63

This is Norman.

He lives in this building.

Pages 64-65

Tom has been kidnapped. The pictures are numbered and arranged in the correct order to show exactly what happened to him.

 1

2

 3

 4

5

6

 7

8

Pages 66-67

Each number stands for a letter, 1=A, 2=B and so on, while numbers are shown as small letters. You need to add punctuation marks for the decoded message to make sense.

Rogue Robot Ship to base on Robotica: Mission to kidnap Earth-thing successful. He will remain deep-frozen for 79 micro-minutes before being taken to the Challenge Chamber at 93:41. End of Message.

Pages 68-69

Izzy is right. There are several differences between the real Tom and this trick one.

Spot on wrong cheek

Wrong-shaped nose

Six fingers

T shirt with long sleeves and white collar

Pages 70-71

The kidnappers' vapour trail is shown in red.

Pages 72-73

All the broken or missing parts and their replacements are numbered in this picture.

To mend the bus, match the number of the broken or missing part with the spare of the same number.

Pages 74-75

The route to Robotica is marked in red. Everything on the map is shown back to front.

The bus is here. ➤

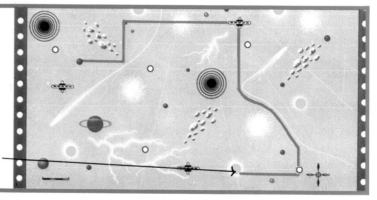

Pages 76-77

As the bus enters the skyway, the time is 93:15. The skyway signpost, the observation bulletin and the dashboard clock all show the same time.

It is 855 mega-miles to the Pluton exit. Here the patrolman stops the bus and the time on his watch reads 93:25. If this was correct, the bus would have travelled at 85.5 mega-miles per micro-minute, breaking the

speed limit for buses of 60 mega-miles per micro-minute.

The time on the dashboard clock is 93:30. It always shows the correct time, so the patrolman's watch must be wrong. This means that Roger drove 855 mega-miles in 15 micro-minutes at an average speed of 57 mega-miles per micro-minute. The bus was not breaking the speed limit.

94

Pages 78-79

If lines are drawn joining the signal landmarks, they form an arrow pointing to the base.

The base is here.

Pages 80-81

This is the sequence with the missing numbers added. The jump between the numbers increases by two each time.

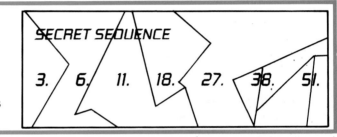

SECRET SEQUENCE

3. 6. 11. 18. 27. 38. 51.

Pages 82-83

Izzy, Roger and Norman are here. Their route to the map is marked in red. The message on page 67 says Tom will be taken to the Challenge Chamber. The only safe route is marked in black.

Pages 84-85

Try to imagine the other side of the keys. The pattern will be reversed.

Key number five is the only one that will open the door to the Challenge Chamber. It only matches the key shape if it is turned over, as shown here.

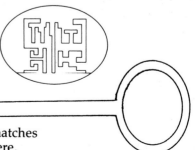

Pages 86-87

This picture shows how to isolate the enemy rockets with three defence discs, and so beat the computer.

Pages 88-89

The route through the laser maze is shown in red.

Page 90

Several things, ringed in black, suggest that Norman and Roger are not far away.

TIME TRAIN TO ANCIENT ROME

Gaby Waters

Illustrated by
Brenda Haw

Designed by Kim Blundell

Map and maze illustrations by
Martin Newton

Contents

About this Story

Time Train to Ancient Rome is an exciting adventure that takes you on a journey backwards through time to the grandeur and intrigues of imperial Rome.

Along the way, there are lots of fun puzzles and tricky problems to solve. Find the answers to these before going on to the next episode in the story.

Look at the pictures carefully and watch out for vital clues and information. Sometimes you will need to flip back through the story to help you find an answer.

There are extra clues on page 139 and you can check your answers on pages 140 to 144.

Just turn the page to begin the adventure...

At the Station

Lucy and Bill ran through the station towards the train on platform number 13. They dashed past the ticket barrier and sprinted down the last flight of steps just as the guard raised his flag. It was then that Lucy noticed several odd things and some even odder people on the platform. She wanted to stop and take a closer look, but there was no time to lose.

How many odd things and people can you spot?

A Strange Journey

They leaped aboard and the guard blew his whistle. The train lurched forward and steamed out of the station.

Bill and Lucy were off to stay with their Uncle Sidney in Grimbledon. Lucy wasn't looking forward to it very much. She gazed out of the window as the train left the town behind and tried not to think about the long, boring days ahead.

All of a sudden, the train plunged into a tunnel and everything went black. The tunnel wasn't very long, but when they reached the other end, the view through the window was somehow different. The trees and the fields were normal enough, but the things and the people looked strangely old-fashioned. And as the train gathered speed, they seemed to grow stranger and older.

They travelled on and on through the unknown landscape until, many hours later, they rounded a sweeping bend and the train began to slow down. Magnificent white stone buildings lined the track as the train wheezed to a halt. Bill and Lucy grabbed their backpacks and made for the door.

103

Arrival

They stepped off the train on to a gleaming, white platform. They knew at once that something was very wrong. Grimbledon Station had never looked like this before.

It was all very odd. Bill and Lucy could hardly believe what they were seeing and hearing. All around them, people were chattering in a strange-sounding language and their clothes were extraordinary.

Where were they and where was Uncle Sidney? Lucy pulled out his letter and read his confusing instructions.

Where should they meet Uncle Sidney?

The Wax Message

Uncle Sidney was nowhere to be seen. They waited ... and waited ... and waited. Then they walked out to the main entrance and looked up and down the street. But there was still no sign of him.

All of a sudden, a boy in a loin cloth sprinted up to them, holding out a brown, leather sack. He thrust it into Bill's hands, said something very fast in a funny foreign language and sped off again.

Lucy untied the sack and emptied the contents onto the ground. There was a scroll of thick paper, a handful of coins, two small, golden charms and a wooden-framed wax slate. Row after row of capital letters were carved into the wax. At first they made no sense at all, but bit by bit, Bill deciphered the strange message.

Can you work out the message on the wax slate?

Here you can see the contents
of the leather sack.

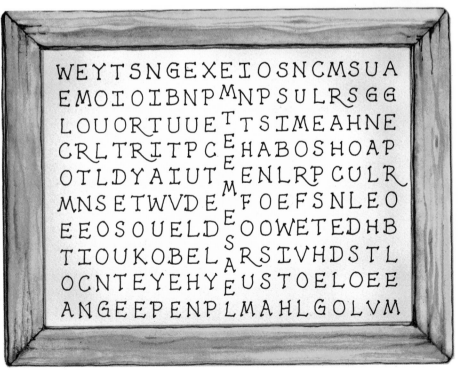

WEYTSNGEXEIOSNCMSUA
EMOIOIBNPMNPSULRSGG
LOUORTUUETTSIMEAHNE
CRLTRITPCEHABOSHOAP
OTLDYAIUTEENLRPCULR
MNSETWVDEMFOEFSNLEO
EEOSOUELDSOOWETEDHB
TIOUKOBELARSIVHDSTL
OCNTEYEHYEUSTOELOEE
ANGEEPENPLMAHLGOLVM

Which Way?

ROME
(FORUM)
ONE AND
A HALF
MILES

Bill was puzzled. Should he believe the wax message or was it some sort of joke? Lucy picked up one of the golden charms and slipped the chain around her neck. All at once, as if by magic, the mysterious foreign chatter turned into words she could speak and understand.

"Now let's find Uncle Sidney," she said in the strange new language, as Bill fastened the other charm around his neck.

They left the station and set off down a cobbled road. They were in the country, but in the distance they saw the walls and buildings of a city. Lucy stopped for a moment and looked around. She delved into the sack, and pulled out the scroll. It was a map.

"We're here," she said, pointing. "We know where we're going, so we just need to find the shortest route."

Which is the shortest route?

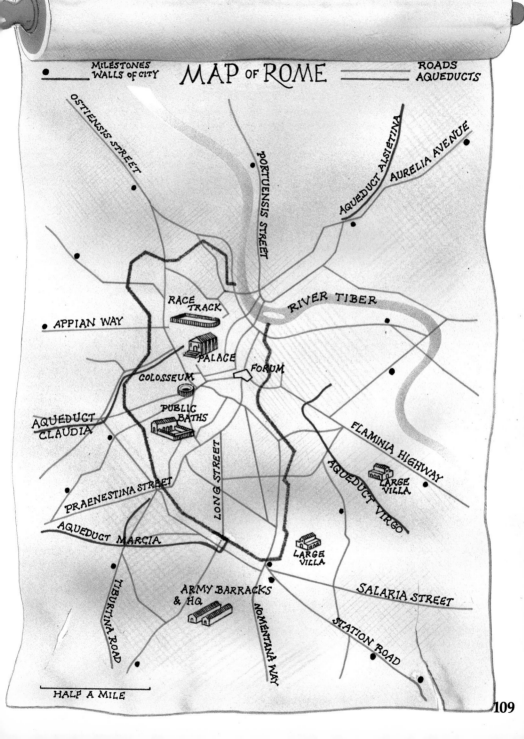

MILESTONES
WALLS OF CITY

MAP of ROME

ROADS
AQUEDUCTS

OSTIENSIS STREET

PORTUENSIS STREET

AQUEDUCT ALSIETINA

AURELIA AVENUE

RACE TRACK

RIVER TIBER

APPIAN WAY

PALACE

FORUM

COLOSSEUM

AQUEDUCT CLAUDIA

PUBLIC BATHS

FLAMINIA HIGHWAY

LARGE VILLA

AQUEDUCT VIRGO

LONG STREET

PRAENESTINA STREET

AQUEDUCT MARCIA

LARGE VILLA

TIBURTINA ROAD

ARMY BARRACKS & HQ.

NOMENTANA WAY

SALARIA STREET

STATION ROAD

HALF A MILE

109

In the Forum

The scroll map led them into a large, open square surrounded by grand-looking buildings. It was packed with people rushing around making a lot of noise.

"This must be the forum," said Lucy. "But where's Uncle Sidney?"

Can you spot Uncle Sidney?

Uncle Sidney and the Soldiers

Lucy spotted Uncle Sidney first. She grabbed Bill's arm and together they dashed across the bustling forum. Uncle Sidney was standing in the middle of a group of mean-looking soldiers, wearing what appeared to be a baggy yellow sheet. He looked very cross and was shouting at the soldiers at the top of his voice.

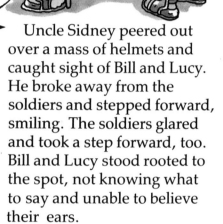

What? Arrest me? Certainly not. I am Sidonius and the Emperor's my friend.

Who are these barbarian brats? Leave or we'll arrest you too.

Billius and Lucilla – my nephew and niece. They've just arrived on the Time Train.

Suddenly, Uncle Sidney grabbed their hands and began to run. He zigzagged back across the forum, leaving the astonished soldiers behind, shouting and waving their spears. Bill and Lucy bombarded their Uncle with questions. But Uncle Sidney said nothing. He smiled mysteriously and kept on running.

Uncle Sidney peered out over a mass of helmets and caught sight of Bill and Lucy. He broke away from the soldiers and stepped forward, smiling. The soldiers glared and took a step forward, too. Bill and Lucy stood rooted to the spot, not knowing what to say and unable to believe their ears.

Sidonius? Billius? I don't understand.

Time train? Barbarians? What's going on?

At last they stopped to catch their breath and Uncle Sidney began to talk. Lucy hoped he might explain why they had arrived in Ancient Rome instead of Grimbledon, but he didn't. Instead, he told them a strange story about the Emperor, Fabulus Caesar, and the terrible things that were happening in Rome . . .

Sorry about the detour but things are bad here in Rome. The Emperor's soldiers are arresting all his old friends and no one is safe.

OUCH! My toe.

All of a sudden, a large pebble hurtled towards them, landing with a thump on Uncle Sidney's foot. Bill picked it up and noticed a series of letters and dots scrawled on its surface. Perhaps it was some sort of message. Uncle Sidney agreed and explained that the letters I, V and X were Roman numbers.

"I is 1, V is 5 and X is 10," he explained. "II is 2, III is 3, XX is 20 and so on. When you see a smaller number in front of a bigger number you subtract it from the bigger one, so IV is 4. When you see a smaller number after a bigger number you add them together, which means VI is 6."

Can you decipher the message on the pebble?

XVI · XII · V · I · XIX · V · VIII ·
V · XII · XVI · XIII · V · IX · I · XII ·
II · V · IX · XIV · VII · VIII · V · XII ·
IV · I · XIX · I · XVI · XVIII · IX · XIX ·
XV · XIV · V · XVIII · XIII · XXV ·
XIV · XXI · XIII · II · V · XVIII · IX ·
XIX · XIV · IX · XIV · V · XX ·
XXV · X IV · IX · XIV · V ·
VI · XVIII · XV · XIII ·
VI · III ·

At the Toga Shop

Bill and Lucy soon decoded the strange message.

"But who's it from?" asked Bill. "And what should we do about it?"

"We must make a plan," said Uncle Sidney, slipping the pebble into his cloak. "But first of all you must get rid of your Barbarian clothes."

Uncle Sidney led them into a small shop jam-packed with bales of cloth, off-the-peg tunics and cut-price cloaks. The shopkeeper stared in amazement at Bill and Lucy's strange clothes while Uncle Sidney explained what they needed.

"A tunic and a toga for Billius," he said. "A stola and a palla for Lucilla, and two pairs of sandals."

The shopkeeper and his assistants set to work, with tape measures, pins and needles. Meanwhile, Uncle Sidney crept out of the shop and set off to discuss the strange pebble message with his friend the sculptor.

In no time at all, Bill and Lucy were outfitted in real Roman clothes. Bill was very pleased with his new outfit, but Lucy wasn't so sure. Her dress was made of funny itchy material and the cloak kept slipping off.

Next the shopkeeper led them into the shoe department at the back of the shop. Bill chose a pair of yellow sport sandals and strutted around the shop admiring his new Roman feet.

Bill pulled out some shining coins from the leather sack and turned round to find the shopkeeper emptying baskets of assorted sandals all over the floor. Lucy was sitting on a bench with one red sandal on her right foot.

"I know I've seen the other one somewhere," said the shopkeeper.

Can you find Lucy's missing sandal?

The Emperor's Head

They found Uncle Sidney in a sculptor's studio just up the road. He was standing in a famous-person position on a low table, keeping very still.

The sculptor's name was Bustamarbellus, or Busta for short. He was hammering away at a great big block of stone which was starting to take the shape of Uncle Sidney's head.

Bill and Lucy gazed at the peculiar collection of stone carvings that crammed the studio. There were horses' heads and human heads, bits of legs and broken toes.

"Who are all these people?" asked Lucy, gazing at a row of stone heads.

"Important Romans," said Uncle Sidney, almost without opening his mouth. "Just like me."

"The Emperor's head is here too," said the sculptor. "It's a perfect likeness. He's the one with the bushy eyebrows and not much hair."

Where is the Emperor's head?

116

Watching the Procession

All of a sudden, the sound of trumpets and people cheering filled the street outside. A procession was passing by. They all dashed upstairs to get a better view.

"It's the Emperor," cried Uncle Sidney, wishing he wasn't so near-sighted.

Bill and Lucy stared at the man in the purple toga. Something was wrong...

"Oh no," gasped Busta. "This can only mean one thing."

What's wrong?

THE SCROLL SHOP

119

Three Soothsayers

One hour later, Uncle Sidney, Bill and Lucy arrived at a cave in a rocky hillside just outside the city. This was the home of the famous three soothsayers. If anybody could help solve the mystery of the Emperor's imposter, they could.

"Ten denarii per consultation," growled the grumpy guard at the entrance.

Bill handed over ten silver coins and the guard led them into a gloomy cave where they found three funny old men sitting on stone blocks.

"A friend of mine has been replaced by an imposter," Uncle Sidney explained. "Do you know what has happened to him?"

Your friend has been kidnapped by a rogue apple seller. Follow the milestones past the fighting gladiators to the steaming thermal springs. Beware the Ides of March.

PHIBBER

The soothsayers gave their answers at once, but to Bill and Lucy's surprise, each one was different.

"Only one of them is telling the truth," growled the guard. "The other two are lying."

"Do they always do this?" asked Lucy, amazed.

"Always," said the guard. "But a different one tells the truth each time."

Lucy gave the guard another ten coins and spoke to the soothsayers.

"Which one of you told Uncle Sidney the truth?" she asked.

Which of the soothsayers is telling the truth this time? Which one told Uncle Sidney the truth?

The Search Begins

They scrambled down the rocky hillside wondering what the soothsayer's cryptic message meant and where to start their search.

"What's a numbered stone?" asked Bill feeling very confused.

"Perhaps it's a milestone," said Uncle Sidney. "Then there's steam in the baths and apple sellers in the er ..."

"Market?" Lucy suggested.

They decided to split up. Bill ran to the baths, Uncle Sidney set off on a milestone search and Lucy headed for the market.

Fifteen minutes and thirty apples later, she was standing in a line. The lady in front was buying enough fruit and vegetables to feed the Roman army and the boy behind the stall was trying hard to work out how much it all cost.

"Hurry up," said the lady, grabbing the boy's wax slate.

Lucy glanced at the slate over the lady's shoulder. She felt sorry for the boy. Roman numbers were hard to add up quickly and Roman money was tricky too – four asses made one sestertius and four sestertii made one denarius.

"It's obvious," said the lady. "It comes to six denarii."

"No it doesn't," cried Lucy.

Is Lucy correct? How much should the lady pay?

PLUMS : VIII S.
LETTUCE : XII A
CABBAGE : XIV A
LEMONS : III S
APPLES : IX A
GRAPES : XV A
EXOTIC FRUIT : II D

TOTAL

Bill Takes a Bath

Roman baths weren't like ordinary baths. Bill hadn't a clue what to do or where to go, so he decided to follow everyone else. He took off his clothes and wrapped himself in a towel. Then he walked through an open area where men were wrestling into a hot room filled with steam.

All of a sudden, he overheard two men talking in low, secretive voices. He thought nothing of it at first, but as he walked into an even hotter, steamier room, his heart sank.

Through the steam he caught the unmistakable sight of a serpent tattooed on to a

124

man's arm. The arm belonged to one of the men he had overheard moments before.

The two men left the steam and Bill followed, listening to all they said. First they went into a room where slaves scraped the dirt off their backs, then they swam in a warm indoor pool followed by a dip in an outdoor pool filled with freezing cold water. By now Bill had heard enough. He had to hurry back and warn the others.

This special picture shows Bill and the two men in each room in the baths. Can you follow their suspicious conversation?

The Gladiators' Show

Meanwhile, back at the market, the fruit boy was beaming. He thanked Lucy over and over again and handed her a juicy red apple and a small disc made of clay.

This was it! The apple seller's gift. But what was it? The boy explained that the disc was a ticket to the gladiators' show at the Colosseum. He pointed to a large, circular building in the distance. Lucy thanked him and sped off to join the crowds heading for the Colosseum.

Lucy handed her ticket to the man at the turnstile, keeping her ears and eyes open for some sort of clue that would lead her to the Emperor.

The show was just about to begin and the first prisoner was led up from the dungeons to fight Daddio Maximus, the gladiator champion.

Several minutes later

The prisoner lunged at his opponent and the crowd began to roar. At the same time, Lucy remembered the soothsayer's words. Suddenly they all made sense and Lucy knew that the Emperor was one of the prisoners waiting to fight the dreaded Daddio Maximus. There was no time to lose.

PRISONERS' NUMBERS	CELL NUMBERS
XIV	XXI
XXVIII	XVIII
XXXI	VI
XLIX	XI
LVI	XIV
LXV	XXV
LXXVII	XXXIV
LXXXIV	IX
XCIX	XL

As she crept towards the dungeons, Lucy spotted a list of numbers on a notice board. One of them was very familiar. In a flash of inspiration, she realized that the pebble message was the "numbered stone" and that it had come from the Emperor.
Which number is familiar?

127

Down to the Dungeons

Lucy slipped through the entrance into a gloomy passage that sloped steeply downward. The air was damp and chilly and the further she went, the darker it became. At the bottom of the slope, she came to a junction with passages running right, left and straight ahead.

The only light came from a flickering candle. Beside it was a slab of intricately carved marble set into the wall. Lucy picked up the candle to take a closer look.

All of a sudden, she realized that the circular pattern in the center of the slab was a plan of the dungeons showing a maze of passages and lots of little cells.

Only five of the cells were numbered, but she was sure that the numbers followed a pattern. If only she could.work out the numbering system, she could locate the Emperor's cell and trace a route to it

What route should Lucy take to get to the Emperor's cell?

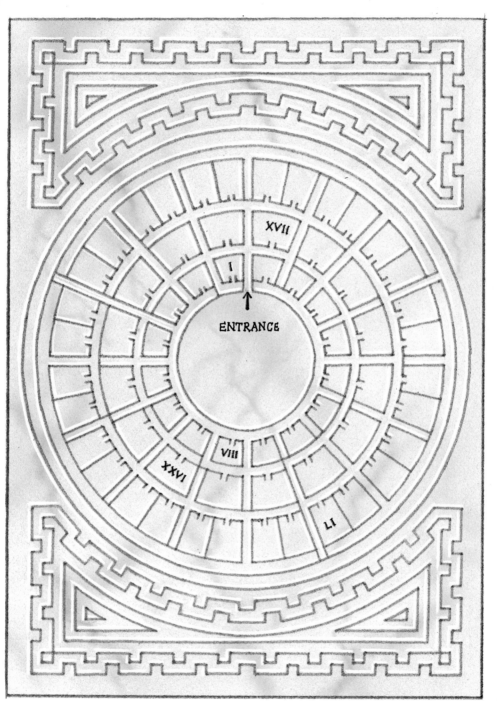

XVII

I

↑
ENTRANCE

VIII

XXVI

LI

The Shattered Slate

Lucy tugged at the rusty bolt and heaved the heavy cell door open to find the Emperor inside, dressed in a gladiator's outfit. He was very surprised to see Lucy. She explained who she was and together they retraced Lucy's route through the dungeons to the entrance into the arena.

Lucy threw her cloak over the Emperor's head as a disguise. Then they slipped silently past the guard into the crowds of cheering spectators. They made a dash for the exit and sprinted through the streets of Rome until they arrived, panting and gasping, at the sculptor's studio.

Been : Banquet at the Emp ace by the ter! He doesn't know that says

See snooping there. We shall not who he

Impos that we are some we're

with the think we're track.

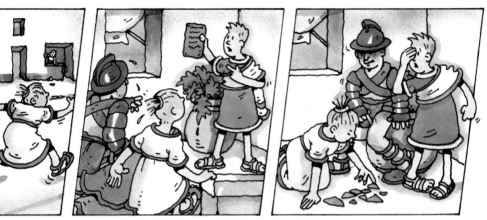

Here they found Bill looking very worried. Uncle Sidney and the sculptor were nowhere to be seen. They had left a message on a clay slate, but Bill couldn't decipher the sculptor's handwriting.

He held up the slate to show them. But suddenly... SMASH!

He dropped it. It fell to the ground and shattered into little pieces.

"It's alright," said Lucy, kneeling down. "We can match all the pieces together."

What does the sculptor's message say?

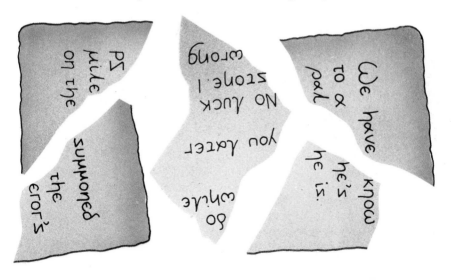

Through the Palace Gardens

Uncle Sidney and the sculptor were in grave danger. There was no time to lose. They had to get to the palace and stop the banquet. But how?

"I know a way into the palace," said the Emperor, smiling. "Quick. Follow me."

He led them through the back streets of Rome to the walls of the palace gardens. Bill and Lucy peered over the wall and the Emperor explained that the door on the far right was always left unlocked.

Now all they needed to do was find a way through the gardens out of sight of the guards.

Can you find a safe route?

133

The Imperial Banquet

Inside the palace, the Emperor led them through a series of magnificent corridors towards the imperial dining room. Bill and Lucy burst into the room, just as the banquet was about to begin.

"STOP!" yelled Bill. "The food is poisoned and the Emperor's a fake."

The two men from the baths glared at Bill, but the fake Emperor just laughed and carried on munching.

Uncle Sidney and the sculptor knew that Bill was telling the truth, but the other guests weren't sure.

Bill did some quick thinking. The only way to convince them was to prove the food was poisoned. And the only way to do that was to offer a plate of poisoned food to the fake Emperor. Bill knew he would refuse. But which dish was poisoned?

Bill thought back to the baths and recalled a strange word. In his mind, he began to rearrange the letters . . .

Which food is poisoned?

Chariot Chase

The fake Emperor's grin became a grimace, and just as Bill expected, he refused the plate of poisoned food. At once, the other guests knew that Bill was telling the truth.

The fake Emperor roared with anger, tossed the plate into the air and kicked over a whole table of food. Bill went flying along with the food and landed with a bump. He sat up, seeing stars, to find Uncle Sidney, the sculptor and the Emperor tying up the fake Emperor's evil accomplices.

Then Lucy spotted the fake Emperor making a quick getaway. She yelled to Bill and the two of them chased after him. Too late. He jumped into an empty chariot and raced away. But Lucy and Bill weren't beaten yet. They sped down the steps to the street and did exactly the same.

"Quick," said Lucy to the driver. "Follow that chariot."

Bill and Lucy clung on tightly as the chariot sped after the fake Emperor out of the city and on to the road that led to the station.

The chariot pulled up on the forecourt. Bill and Lucy leapt out and rushed into the station which was packed with people.

"There he is," cried Bill. "We've got to catch him before it's too late."

Where is he?

What Happened Next

Lucy and Bill jumped aboard in hot pursuit. But all of a sudden, the door slammed shut behind them with a bang and the train lurched forwards with a sudden jolt...

The next thing they knew, the train was slowing down at a station. Bill opened his eyes, feeling very bleary and confused. The train stopped and everyone got out.

Bill and Lucy walked across the platform in a daze –

straight into the arms of Uncle Sidney! He greeted them with a wink and led them away without a word. Lucy didn't know what to think. Was it all a dream? She looked down at her feet – perhaps not. But if it wasn't a dream...

She turned round to look at the train for the last time and smiled as she caught sight of the fake Emperor in the midst of the crowded platform..

Can you see the fake Emperor?

GRIMBLEDON STATION

WANTED
for ancient
crimes

138

Clues

Pages 100-101
This is easy. Use your eyes.

Pages 104-105
Uncle Sidney is describing the station from the opposite direction. A sundial is used to tell the time.

Pages 106-107
Read the first column of letters downwards and the second column upwards, and so on.

Pages 108-109
The milestone pinpoints their position. Use a ruler or a piece of thread to find the shortest route.

Pages 110-111
Remember Uncle Sidney wears glasses.

Pages 112-113
Try replacing the numbers with letters. Here are the Roman numbers 1 to 26.

I	II	III	IV	V	VI
VII	VIII	IX	X	XI	XII
XIII	XIV	XV	XVI	XVII	XVIII
XIX	XX	XXI	XXII	XXIII	XXIV
XXV	XXVI				

Pages 114-115
Look for a sandal of the same size, shape and colour as the one on Lucy's right foot.

Pages 116-117
This is easy. Use your eyes.

Pages 118-119
Compare the Emperor's face with the stone head on pages 116-117.

Pages 120-121
This is very tricky. Look at the answers to Lucy's question. Then test each soothsayer's answer in turn to see if he could be telling the truth while the other two are lying.

Pages 122-123
A = asses, D = denarii, S = sestertii.

Pages 124-125
Look for the sign of the serpent.

Pages 126-127
Look at the pebble message on pages 112-113. L is 50 and C is 100 in Roman numerals.

Pages 128-129
The inner circle of cells are numbered anticlockwise.

Pages 130-131
Trace the shattered bits or photocopy the page and cut them out. Then piece them together.

Pages 132-133
They can crawl behind hedges and use plants as cover to keep out of the guards' sight.

Pages 134-135
Look for the strange word in the suspicious conversation on pages 124-125. Rearrange the letters to find out which food is poisoned.

Pages 136-137
This is easy. Look for the soles of his shoes.

Page 138
Look for the Emperor's face.

Answers

Pages 100-101

The strange things and people are ringed in black.

Pages 104-105

Bill and Lucy should meet Uncle Sidney beneath the sundial. This is a sort of clock which uses a shadow cast by the sun to show the time. Uncle Sidney's right and left are reversed because he is describing the station from the opposite direction.

Pages 106-107

The letters in the wax message read downwards in the first column, upwards in the second column and so on. This is what it says:

WELCOME TO ANCIENT ROME. YOU'LL SOON GET USED TO IT. SORRY TO KEEP YOU WAITING BUT I'VE BEEN HELD UP UNEXPECTEDLY. PLEASE MEET ME IN THE FORUM AS SOON AS POSSIBLE.

LOVE, UNCLE S.

PS THE GOLDEN CHARMS SHOULD SOLVE THE LANGUAGE PROBLEM.

Pages 108-109

The shortest route to the forum is marked in black.

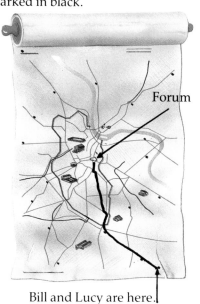

Forum

Bill and Lucy are here.

Pages 110-111

Here is Uncle Sidney.

Pages 112-113

Each number stands for a letter. I(1)=A, II(2)=B and so on. Here is the message with spaces and punctuation marks added.

Please help me. I am being held as a prisoner. My number is ninety nine. From F.C.

Pages 114-115

The missing sandal is ringed in black.

Pages 116-117

The Emperor's head is ringed in black.

Pages 118-119

The Emperor's face, particularly his nose, is not the same as the stone head on pages 116-117. This must mean that the man wearing the Emperor's clothes is not the Emperor, but an imposter.

The Emperor's stone head   The imposter

Pages 120-121

Fraudum is telling Lucy the truth. This means that Phibber is lying to Lucy which in turn means that Fraudum lied to Uncle Sidney. Spurius is also lying to Lucy which means that the opposite of what he says to her is the truth. In other words, Spurius DID answer Uncle Sidney's question truthfully.

(If you got this one right, you're a genius.)

Pages 122-123

The total comes to 50 asses, 22 sestertii and 2 denarii. This is equal to 9 denarii, 3 sestertii and 2 asses. The lady is trying to get away with paying less than she owes.

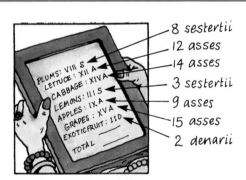

PLUMS: VIII S A — 8 sestertii
LETTUCE: XII A — 12 asses
CABBAGE: XIV A — 14 asses
LEMONS: III S — 3 sestertii
APPLES: IX A — 9 asses
GRAPES: XV A — 15 asses
EXOTIC FRUIT: II D — 2 denarii
TOTAL

Pages 124-125

You can spot the two men holding the suspicious conversation by the serpent signs tattooed on their arms. Here is their suspicious conversation:

"The banquet is arranged.
All the guests will die."
"When?"
"Today."
"At the palace?"
"Correct."
"Where's the poison?"
"It's only in the HUMMOROSS.
Get it?"
"I see."

Pages 126-127

The number 99 is familiar. In his pebble message on pages 112-113, the Emperor says that he is a prisoner with the number 99. The notice board shows that prisoner number 99 is in cell number 40.

Pages 128-129

Lucy's route is shown in black.

Pages 130-131

When the shattered slate is pieced together, the message reads as follows:

We have been summoned to a banquet at the palace by the Emperor's imposter! He doesn't know that we know that he's not who he says he is. We shall do some snooping while we're there. See you later.

PS No luck with the milestone. I think we're on the wrong track.

Pages 132-133

The safe route through the gardens is marked in black.

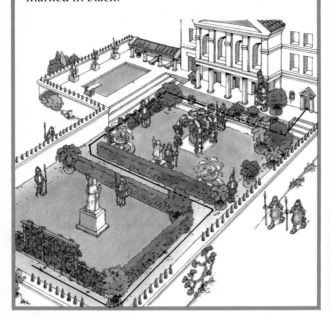

Pages 134-135

The crooks in the baths said that only the HUMMOROSS were poisoned. If you rearrange the letters, this word becomes MUSHROOMS.

Pages 136-137

Here is the fake Emperor.

Page 138

Like Bill and Lucy, the fake Emperor is now in modern clothes.

First published in 1988 by Usborne Publishing Ltd, Usborne House, 83-85 Saffron Hill, London EC1N 8RT, England.

Copyright © 1988 Usborne Publishing Ltd.

The name Usborne and the device are Trade Marks of Usborne Publishing Ltd.

Printed in Belgium.   American edition 1988.